W9-AHR-866

'OHANA MEANS FAMILY

ILIMA LOOMIS

ILLUSTRATED BY KENARD PAK

NEAL PORTER BOOKS
HOLIDAY HOUSE / NEW YORK

For my mom, Paula —I.L.

To Millie —K.P.

Neal Porter Books

Text copyright © 2020 by Ilima Loomis
Illustrations copyright © 2020 by Kenard Pak
All Rights Reserved
HOLIDAY HOUSE is registered in the U.S. Patent and Trademark Office.
Printed and bound in September 2019 at Toppan Leefung, DongGuan City, China.
The artwork for this book was created with watercolor, gouache, and digital art.
Book design by Jennifer Browne
www.holidayhouse.com
First Edition
1   3   5   7   9   10   8   6   4   2

Library of Congress Cataloging-in-Publication Data

Names: Loomis, Ilima, author. | Pak, Kenard, illustrator.
Title: Ohana means family / written by Ilima Loomis ; pictures by Kenard Pak.
Description: New York : Holiday House, 2020. | "Neal Porter Books."
Summary: In this cumulative rhyme in the style of "The House That Jack
Built," a family celebrates Hawaii and its culture while serving poi at a luau.
Identifiers: LCCN 2019010707 | ISBN 9780823443260 (hardcover)
Subjects: | CYAC: Stories in rhyme. | Luaus—Fiction. | Poi—Fiction.
Hawaii—Fiction.
Classification: LCC PZ8.3.L86193 Oh 2020 | DDC [E]—dc23
LC record available at https://lccn.loc.gov/2019010707

This is the poi
for our ʻohana's lūʻau.

This is the kalo
to make the poi
for our 'ohana's lū'au.

This is the mud
that grows the kalo
to make the poi
for our ʻohana's lūʻau.

This is the water, clear and cold,
that covers the mud
that grows the kalo
to make the poi
for our ʻohana's lūʻau.

These are the hands, so wise and old
that reach through the water, clear and cold,
into the mud
to pick the kalo
to make the poi
for our ʻohana's lūʻau.

This is the land that's never been sold,
where work the hands so wise and old,
that reach through the water, clear and cold,
into the mud
to pick the kalo
to make the poi
for our 'ohana's lū'au.

This is the stream of sunlit gold,
flooding the land that's never been sold,
where work the hands so wise and old,
that reach through the water, clear and cold,
into the mud
to pick the kalo
to make the poi
for our 'ohana's lū'au.

This is the rain in the valley fold,
that feeds the stream of sunlit gold,
flooding the land that's never been sold,
where work the hands so wise and old,
that reach through the water, clear and cold,

into the mud
to pick the kalo

to make the poi
for our 'ohana's lū'au.

This is the wind on which stories are told,
that lifts the rain to the valley fold,
that feeds the stream of sunlit gold,
flooding the land that's never been sold,
where work the hands so wise and old,
that reach through the water, clear and cold,

into the mud
to pick the kalo
to make the poi
for our 'ohana's lū'au.

This is the sun, all bright and bold,
that warms the wind on which stories are told,
that lifts the rain to the valley fold,
that feeds the stream of sunlit gold,
flooding the land that's never been sold,
where work the hands so wise and old,
that reach through the water, clear and cold,

into the mud
to pick the kalo
to make the poi
for our ʻohana's lūʻau.

This is 'ohana, the loved ones we hold,
who give thanks for the sun, all bright and bold,
that warms the wind on which stories are told,
that lifts the rain to the valley fold,

that feeds the stream of sunlit gold,
flooding the land that's never been sold,
where work the hands so wise and old,
that reach through the water, clear and cold,

into the mud
to pick the kalo
to make the poi

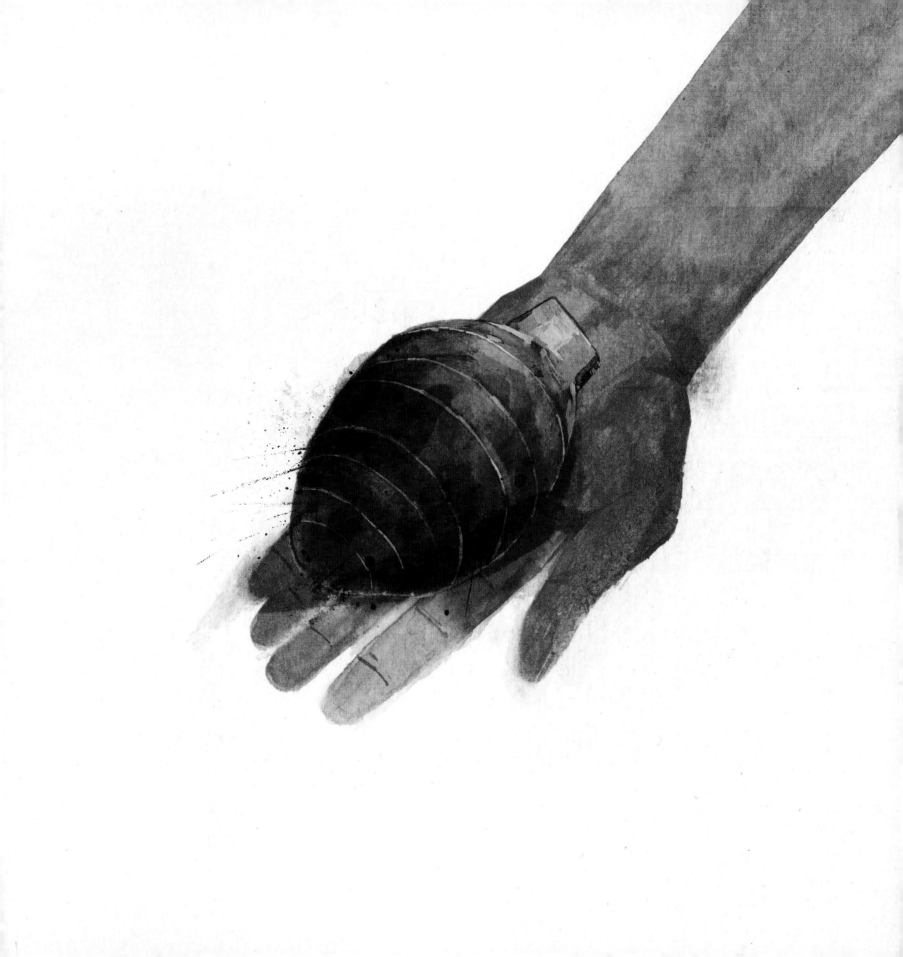

for our ʻohana's lūʻau.

A NOTE ON KALO AND POI

The origin of kalo, also known as taro, is directly connected to the genealogy of the Hawaiian people. In a story passed down from generation to generation, Wākea—the Sky Father—and Hoʻohokukalani gave birth to a stillborn child and buried him near their home. From their infant's earthen grave grew a kalo plant, which they named Hāloanakalaukapalili, meaning "quivering long stalk and leaf." Later, a second child was born and named Hāloa; he became the first kanaka, or Hawaiian. This is why kalo is not just considered a plant, but honored as the elder brother of the human race.

Hawaiians cultivated kalo for more than a thousand years, and they continue to do so today, in both irrigated ponds, called loʻi kalo, and in gardens, called māla ʻai. Hawaiians grew more than 400 varieties of kalo, each having unique characteristics, tastes, and uses. Kalo is a highly nutritious food, and all parts of the plant are eaten—from leaf to corm.

The most common way of eating kalo is pounded into a smooth paste, called poi. To make poi, the corm is steamed and pounded into a mash, called paʻi ʻai, with a stone pounder, called pōhaku kuʻi ʻai, on a wooden board, called papa kuʻi ʻai. When the paʻi ʻai becomes smooth, it is placed into a calabash, called an ʻumeke, and mixed with small amounts of water to become poi.

Poi was the staple food of Hawaiians, and it is still cherished today. ʻOhana put their conflicts aside when poi is present, because it is considered disrespectful to quarrel in front of elders. Poi is often the first food given to babies, and no celebratory lūʻau is complete without it.

—Hōkūao Pellegrino
Nohoʻana Farm
Waikapū, Maui, Hawaiʻi

A NOTE FROM THE AUTHOR

It is through a shared meal that we come together as a family. An ʻohana can include not just parents, children, brothers, and sisters, but also neighbors, visitors, and friends old and new. Food connects us—not just with one another, but with the whole world. The land, the water, the air, our community, and even the sun come together in every bite. It is this connection that I hoped to honor when I sat down to write about the most traditional Hawaiian food, poi.

—Ilima Loomis

GLOSSARY

Kalo – the taro plant, *Colocasia esculenta*

Kanaka – human being, man, person, Hawaiian

Loʻi kalo – wetland pond, used for cultivating kalo

Lūʻau – a Hawaiian feast, this word is also used to describe the cooked kalo leaf

Māla ʻai – garden, cultivated field, usually rain fed

ʻOhana – family, relative

Paʻi ʻai – hard, hand-pounded kalo

Papa kuʻi ʻai – the wooden board on which kalo is pounded

Pōhaku kuʻi ʻai – the stone tool used for pounding kalo

Poi – the starchy paste made from the cooked corm of the kalo plant, a staple Hawaiian food

ʻUmeke – bowl made from calabash gourd or wood